Mother-daughter duo, Sally
Gardner and Lydia Corry are keen
conservationists. Sally is a Costa and
Carnegie-winning author and Lydia's
Eight Princesses and a Magic Mirror
was a *Guardian* Book of the Year 2019.
Tho Floating Moon is the fourth book
in this series following *The Tindims of
Rubbish Island*, *The Tindims and the
Turtle Tangle* and *The Tindims and the
Ten Green Bottles*.

The TINDIMS

and the Floating Moon

Sally Gardner & Lydia Corry

ZEPHYR

an imprint of Head of Zeus

Head of Zeus Ltd
First Floor East
5-8 Hardwick Street
London EC1R 4RG

www.headofzeus.com

To Nathan
with all our love.

SG and LC

hello!

Chapter One

Where Spokes comes up with a plan, but Pinch isn't so sure.

The Tindims call autumn 'driftsea'. It's a time of mists and fogs. When Roo-Roo trees lose their leaves and strange rubbish is found washed up in Turtle Bay. It's a time to make sure that roofs aren't leaking, and that windows and doors don't rattle.

This driftsea, thanks to Spokes' brain-wave, each house had a phone. Something they had never had before. Spokes had the idea after the adventure of the ten green bottles. He said all this getting lost malarkey had to stop. It was most worrying not knowing where everyone was.

'There aren't that many Tindims in the first place,' he said. 'We can't afford to go losing each other willy-nilly.'

As Barnacle Bow had
helped Spokes with the
design for the old cable car
that used to run from his
and Granny Gull's houseboat
to Captain Spoons' house,
Spokes asked for his help
again. Together they designed
a simple Tindim phone system.
It was better by far than the old
tin phone which Spokes used to talk to
Captain Spoons in the wheelhouse.

Putting in a new phone system involved
a lot of digging.

And that is where Pinch, Skittle's furry
purry pet, found Spokes... down a hole.

'Why are you down a hole? You are not a mole. Oh, that rhymes, actually,' said Pinch.

'I am putting in a phone system,' said Spokes. 'So, if you want to speak to Skittle you can call her and tell her where you are.'

'Why would I want to do that?' asked Pinch. 'Most of the time she's right next to me and I can see where she is.'

'Well, if not Skittle, Granny Gull, perhaps,' suggested Spokes.

'Why would I do that, when I can run over and say hello?' asked Pinch.

Spokes didn't have any more answers, but he did have a lot of holes to dig.

Pinch wandered off to look for Skittle
and Brew. But then an urgent thought
came to him and he rushed back to find
Spokes.

'Spokes,' he called.
He couldn't see him
anywhere. He looked
down one hole and then
another, until finally he
found Spokes having a
break and a cup of glee
with Barnacle Bow.

'The thing is,' said Pinch, 'Tindims don't get lost on Rubbish Island, it's only when we leave the island that trouble begins.'

Spokes smiled. 'I have thought of that,' he said and pointed up to the treehouse. At the very top was a pole sticking out through the branches and into the sky.

'What is that?' asked Pinch.

'It is a wireless mast and it should pick up a Tindim signal.' Spokes took one of his natty designed phones and pressed a few buttons.

'Who are you calling?' asked Pinch.

'You will see,' said Spokes.

Chapter Two

Where they make an
important phone call
and hear that a Gupper
fog might be coming
their way. But what
is a Gupper fog?

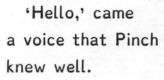

S pokes tapped in the numbers and handed the phone to Pinch.

'Hello,' came a voice that Pinch knew well.

'Is that you, Tiddledim the explorer?' Pinch asked.

'Yes, who else could it be?'

'You mean, I am talking to you, on your ship?'

'Yes.'

'You, who set sail from Rubbish Island a week ago?' said Pinch.

'That me, the one and only,' said Tiddledim. 'I am as far away and further than you can throw a custard pie.'

'Have you ever thrown a custard pie?'
asked Pinch.

'Yes, I have indeed,' said Tiddledim.
'Now, young Pinch, put me on speaker
phone so that Spokes and Barnacle Bow
can hear me. How's it going, Spokes?'
asked Tiddledim.

'I should have all the phones connected
in a matter of days,' said Spokes.

'Good,' said Tiddledim. 'Just thought you should know, I saw what looks like a Gupper fog. Hopefully it won't come your way.'

'Hope not,' said Barnacle Bow.

'What is a Gupper fog?' asked Pinch.

'Well,' said Tiddledim. 'The fog is named after the Gupper squid, which can only move from salt water to fresh water when it is wrapped up in a fog. No one knows which came first, the squid or the fog.'

Sounds like a riddle.

Sounds like a pickle.

Sounds fishy.

'Don't worry. You would know soon
enough if you had one,' said Tiddledim.

'How?' said Pinch.

'They can hang around a bit because
they don't like leaving their squid. Now I
must be going. Toodle pip, goodbye.'

'Wow,' said Pinch. 'That is brilliant.
Now I see why every house needs a
phone. So we can all speak to Tiddledim
the explorer.'

'That's not the only reason,' said
Spokes.

'Oh,' said Pinch.
'Have you ever seen a
Gupper squid?'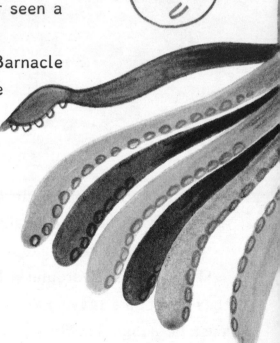

'Yes,' said Barnacle
Bow. 'We have
one in the
lake and
that one
came
wrapped
in a Gupper
fog.'

'Did you see
it happen?'
'No, but the
light the squid
gives off can be
seen at moontide.'
'It must be a bit
lonely,' said Pinch.
'What does it look like?'
Barnacle Bow went and
found a picture in a book.
'Look, the Gupper squid has
two large eyes and eight arms
and two tentacles that light up.'
'That's a squid? I wouldn't
want that in our lake,' said Pinch.
'You mustn't judge a squid on its
looks alone,' said Barnacle Bow.

It was on Tunaday
when, finally, all the
phones were connected.
By then they had
forgotten about
the Gupper fog.

Skittle, Pinch and
Brew, who were up in
the treehouse, were
the first to make a
call on the brand-
new completed phone
system. They decided to
call Captain Spoons and ask if
he could bring over some Roo-Roo cakes.

Hitch Stitch called Spokes to
congratulate him and Barnacle Bow on
their phone system. Ethel B Dina phoned
Tiddledim the explorer, who said he would
be out of touch for a week or so, as

he'd be busy exploring
and wouldn't have time to
answer the phone.

Admiral Bonnet spoke to Mug, and
Mug spoke to Granny Gull
about knitting patterns.
Although it was good
to hear each other's
voices, it wasn't the
same as actually being
with one another and
having glee and Roo-Roo
muffins.

After a week or so they forgot about
the phones and just when they were sure
they would never need to use them again,
something happened that proved how
useful a phone could be. A fog arrived.
No one could be sure exactly what
kind of fog it was. Spokes tried to call
Tiddledim to ask if this was indeed the
fog he'd been talking about. But there
was no reply. As for the fog, it clung,
limpet-tight, to Rubbish Island.

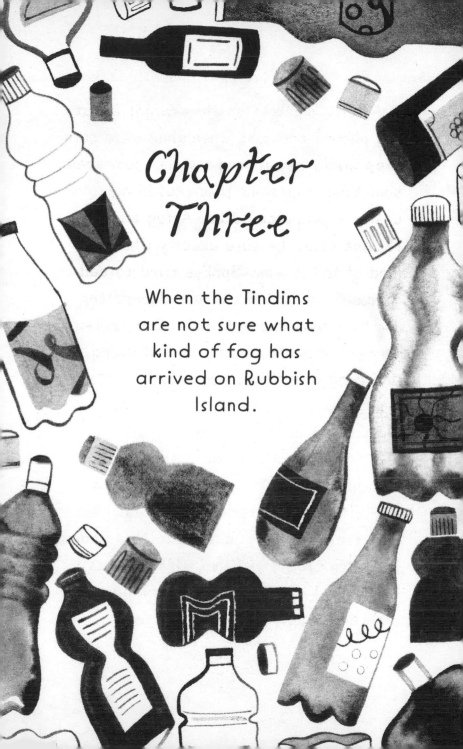

Chapter Three

When the Tindims are not sure what kind of fog has arrived on Rubbish Island.

This fog was a thick, greyish
fog that smelled of old socks.
It came, unseen in the night,
and hung over the Lake of Still Waters.
Spokes was certain that it was the
Gupper fog and he hoped it would go
away. But the fog became thicker and
thicker until it was the worst fog that
any Tindim could remember. It wasn't a
Sea Fret fog; they just tickle the ground
and then blow away. No, this fog was
heavy, and it clutched to every single bit
of Rubbish Island, refusing to let go.

It drifted into Hitch Stitch's house
and hung out there, feeling sorry for
itself. It tried to hide in Skittle's house.
Captain Spoons chased it away with a
frying pan. Baby Cup thought it was a
friend and invited it in, before Mug shoo-
shooed it away.

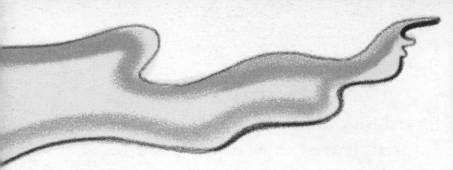

The fog sneaked into Spokes' engine
room, but Spokes was too fast for it
and brushed it away. Still it refused to
leave and the Tindims were well and truly
stuck. They couldn't steer the island
back, as they couldn't see where back
was, and they couldn't go forward, as
they couldn't see which way forward was.

This was bothersome. After all, it was
driftsea, the season for surprises. Often
strange and wonderful things would wash
up on the beach at this time of year.
Except this driftsea, there was no point
keeping a lookout because there was
nothing to see but fog, fog, fog, which
watched through the window as Skittle
and her family had lunch.

'Do you see a squid eye in that fog?' asked Skittle.

'Yes,' said Pinch. 'I see four eyes and *that's a fact.*'

'Then it is a Gupper fog,' said Admiral Bonnet. 'I hear that they are the very worst because they won't leave.'

'Why won't they leave?' asked Skittle.

'The fog doesn't want to say goodbye to the squid because it's its only friend and it doesn't have a home to go to.'

'Have you ever seen a Gupper squid before?' asked Skittle.

'Yes, they have arms which light up,'
said Admiral Bonnet. 'But I'll tell you
this for a bag of shark's teeth, this fog,
just like a Gupper fog, shows no sign
of going. And all I can say to that is
trumpets and tin hats.'

'Never a truer word said, my Admiral
of the Seven Seas, and the love of a
Spoons' life,' said Captain Spoons.

Admiral Bonnet blushed.

Pinch said, 'And *that's a fact.*'

'It is a good thing,' said Admiral Bonnet, 'that we each have a phone and can talk to one another, even if we can't see each other. Without it we would be in much more of a pickle pie and no mistake.'

They were serving pudding, which is their favourite part of the meal. It had become so gloomy and foggy inside that Captain Spoons had to light a candle to find the pudding bowls. That's when the phone rang.

It was Ethel B Dina, who was in a bit of a state.

'Oh, my still and sparkling darlings, do you hear that?'

'Hear what?' asked Admiral Bonnet.

'The man in the moon is singing,' said Ethel B Dina.

'We wouldn't be able to hear him all the way down here on Rubbish Island. Are you sure you are all right, my old lifesaver?' asked Admiral Bonnet. 'The moon is miles and miles away, up in the sky.'

'That's the trouble,' said Ethel B Dina. 'I don't mean to panic you, but I think the moon has fallen into the sea. I can hear it humming the tune to a song we sing.'

'What song?' said Admiral Bonnet.

'You know.'

'No, I don't.'

'The one we sing at the Brightsea
Festival.

Hey, Skittle diddle!
The cup and the fiddle,
Brew jumped over the moon.
Oh, how Pinch did laugh,
To see such fun,
While Jug ran away with Broom.

'Except it is singing different words to
the same tune.'

Chapter Four

Where Ethel B Dina is worried by what she sees in the water.

That hightide
Granny Gull
and Barnacle Bow
had to light a candle too,
just like Captain Spoons had
done, as the fog had taken away the sun.

'It seems odd, this fog,' said Granny
Gull. 'It's a bit more than a little
nuisance.'

Just then they saw something round
and full of light floating in the sea.

'What is that?' said Granny Gull.

'Well, flip me a clam,' said Barnacle
Bow.

The phone rang.

'My still and sparkling darlings,' said
Ethel. 'Things have gone from worse to
worst. The man in the moon is
still singing and floating in
the sea.'

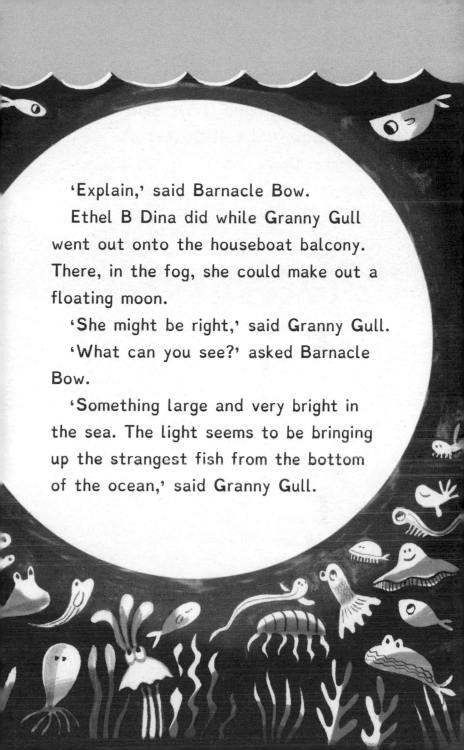

'Explain,' said Barnacle Bow.

Ethel B Dina did while Granny Gull went out onto the houseboat balcony. There, in the fog, she could make out a floating moon.

'She might be right,' said Granny Gull.

'What can you see?' asked Barnacle Bow.

'Something large and very bright in the sea. The light seems to be bringing up the strangest fish from the bottom of the ocean,' said Granny Gull.

'This doesn't sound right,' said
Barnacle Bow. 'I'll call Spokes and we'll
investigate. Don't worry, my old socks,'
he said to Ethel. 'I will call you back
when we have some news.'

He tried to call Spokes, but the line
was busy, so he decided to see for
himself what was going on. 'I won't be
long,' he said bravely to Granny Gull.

First, he tied a light around his head, then he packed two more torches in his rucksack. He grabbed a large ball of string and tied one end to the houseboat. He held tight to the ball as it unwound, so he would always be able to find his way home.

'Oh, twinkle, you went and left me.
Now I see you in the floodtide,
Sparkling in the shallows of the sea.'

It took him quite some time in the
fog to make his way towards Turtle Bay.
He tripped over rocks and slipped into
pools. It was much harder going than
he'd thought. Once he reached the bay
he could faintly hear singing coming
towards him.

There were other words which sounded
as if they weren't that far away. Barnacle

'Oh, twinkle, you went and left me.
Now I see you in the moontide.'

Bow stood still; he could see nothing
in the fog except a glow of light in
the water. And the singing came closer
and closer.

Barnacle Bow's heart started to
beat faster. Out of the fog came a
monster, all lit up. But the minute the
singing monster saw Barnacle Bow, it
too disappeared.

'Hello,' he called. 'It's Barnacle Bow. Who's there?'

'It is me, Spokes.'

'Where are you going?' asked Barnacle Bow.

'I was coming to find you and I thought it might be best to sing my twinkle song as it always makes me feel brave. Did you speak to Ethel B Dina?'

'Yes, and she thinks the moon has fallen into the sea,' said Barnacle Bow. 'That's why I'm here.'

They both stood looking at each other and burst out laughing.

'It seems,' said Spokes, 'we have two problems on our hands. One, the moon, and two, the fog. I am certain, as certain as a circle is round, that this is a Gupper fog.'

'But first, how do we get the moon back in the sky?' asked Barnacle Bow. 'And then how do we get the fog to go away?'

Chapter Five

Where Spokes and Barnacle Bow find treasure on the beach. And they wonder if the Gupper fog has been listening to what they have been saying.

They stood on the beach looking into nothing and agreed how sad it was that they couldn't see what this year's driftsea had brought them.

'Oh, blasted socks!' said Barnacle Bow.

Then a strange thing happened. It was as if the fog had heard them because it lifted its skirt, just high enough for the beach to be seen.

There, gently lapped by the waves, was a big empty barrel and a plastic, see-through dome. It took the two of them, working together, to roll the barrel up the beach. Then they went back for the dome.

'You know,' said Barnacle Bow, 'where
there are two things washed up, there's
bound to be a third.'

They decided to go back to the beach
to have a look.

It was getting late when Spokes
stubbed his toe on something hard. 'Oh,
spanners and hammers,' he said loudly.

He looked down to see, half-buried in
the sand, the rudder of a boat, tangled
up with rope.

'I told you there would be three
things,' said Barnacle Bow.

It was only then that he noticed he
had dropped the ball of string which
he needed to show him the
way home.

'Oh dear,' he said.

'Never mind,' said Spokes. 'Remember, you can always call Granny Gull to explain what's happened, once we reach Hitch Stitch's. After all, we have a phone.'

They were very pleased when at last they saw Hitch Stitch's door and even more pleased to see Hitch Stitch herself.

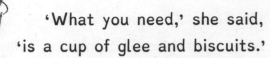

'What you need,' she said,
'is a cup of glee and biscuits.'

The Tindims do tea properly, with
napkins and tablecloths and stiff upper
lips. They think a stiff upper lip might be
useful for eating rock cakes. Not that
any Tindim has a clue what a rock cake,
or a stiff upper lip is.

Barnacle Bow called Granny Gull to
tell her he was safe.

'You know,' he said, as he sat down
again, 'without your phone system we
would be lost.'

'Come on,' said Hitch Stitch, 'let's
play Turn to Treasure with what you've
found.'

'Yes,' agreed Spokes.

This is a game they played with
anything that they found washed up on
the beach. Especially when they weren't

quite sure what it could be used for.
The Tindims' motto is: 'Rubbish today is
treasure tomorrow.'

'A house for Pinch,' said Hitch Stitch.

'A big flowerpot for Broom,' said
Barnacle Bow.

Spokes didn't have his heart in the game. He was too worried about the Gupper fog and the moon. 'You know,' he said, 'we should give Ethel a ring. Someone needs to go and speak to the squid in the Lake of Still Waters and there's only one Tindim who can speak Squid, and that is Ethel B Dina.'

Chapter Six

Where Skittle and
Pinch go out to play
and they too become
lost in the fog.

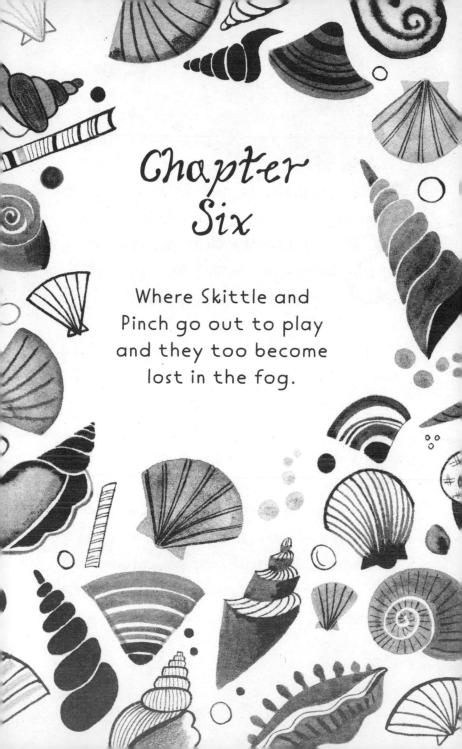

S kittle and Pinch were bored of
being stuck indoors.
'Can't we go out and play?'
asked Skittle.

'I do need to stretch my legs and wag
my tail,' said Pinch.

Captain Spoons was seated by the
fire, dozing.

'I know,' said Admiral Bonnet. 'I will
tie a long piece of string to you both, so
you won't get lost.' And she went to find
two balls of string.

She tied one to Pinch's waistcoat and
the other to Skittle's belt. 'Now don't be
long,' said Admiral Bonnet.

Being outside wasn't quite as jolly
as they'd hoped, because the moment
they started walking away, Skittle's
house vanished in the fog. Then Pinch
disappeared too. The only way they could
make sure they didn't lose each other was
if Skittle held tight to Pinch's tail.

'The one game we can play in the fog is
hide and seek,' said Pinch.

'But,' said Skittle, 'that game doesn't
work without the seeking bit, and in order
to seek we need to be able to see, which
we can't in all this fog.'

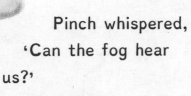

Pinch whispered,
'Can the fog hear
us?'

'No,' said Skittle. 'Why?'

'Because I think the fog likes hiding
things.'

'That's silly, of course it doesn't, it's a
fog,' said Skittle.

Skittle was trying to find the string
connected to Pinch but had become
tangled up in another piece of string.
When she pulled it, instead of Pinch
there was Brew.

'Do you know,' said Brew, 'this string
idea isn't all that good,
as ideas go.'

'No, it's not,'
said Skittle.
'Once Pinch
comes back,
we would
do better to
untangle ourselves and tie
the string to a Roo-Roo tree.'

'Yes,' said Pinch, who suddenly
appeared out of the fog. 'I can always
sniff out a Roo-Roo tree. By the way, I
won that game and *that's a fact.*'

Skittle thought there was
no point arguing and
they set off with a
hop and a skip.
Then they came
across Broom.

'I've just had a call from Ethel B Dina. She's asked me to come over,' said Broom.

'This is where my nose will come in handy,' said Pinch.

At last, the bedraggled little group found Ethel B Dina's door. They were wet as well as cold, and with chattering teeth they rang the bell.

'Wallabangosluth,' said Ethel, as she opened the door. 'Oh, my still and sparkling darlings, are you lost?'

'No,' said Skittle. 'Not now we've found you. What does "wallabangosluth" mean?'

'It means hello in Squid,' said Ethel. 'I thought I would go and ask the squid what it knows about the Gupper fog.'

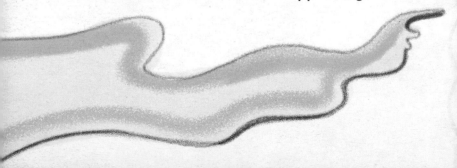

'Where's the moon?' asked Brew when they were dry.

Ethel B Dina guided them to the underwater viewing platform and there it was in the sea, a huge moony ball, glittering in the darkness. All around it were the strangest fish any of them had ever seen.

'Wow,' said Brew. 'Where did those fish come from?'

'They must have been attracted by the light of the moon. I have never seen fish such as these before.'

'Are you sure it is the moon?' asked
Skittle. 'I mean, it does look a bit on the
small side.'

'Perhaps,' said Ethel B Dina, 'it shrank
when it fell in the water. It can happen
with clothes, so maybe the moon is the
same, it shrinks in the wash.'

There was
a knock on
Ethel's door,
and there was
Barnacle Bow,
holding a see-
through plastic
dome.

'What have you
there?' asked Ethel.

'Driftsea treasure,' said Barnacle Bow.

Hitch Stitch came in, pulling a rudder,
followed by Spokes,
who could hardly
be seen behind
the barrel.

'We thought,' said Barnacle Bow, 'you might like to play Turn to Treasure.'

Over another pot of glee, Spokes told them what they had come up with so far. Skittle, Pinch and Brew looked at the barrel, the see-through dome and the rudder, and Brew said, 'A submarine!'

'Why, that is just the label,' said Spokes. 'If we had a submarine, we could rescue the moon and once it has dried out a bit, it might float back into the night sky.'

'And *that's a fact*,' said Pinch.

Chapter Seven

Where Skittle,
Brew and Pinch have
a sleepover and
Barnacle Bow and
Spokes go walking
at moontide.

That ebbtide, Broom took the tired little Tindims over to Brew's house for supper. It was easier to go back there, than try, in the fog, to get back to Skittle's house.

Mug called Captain Spoons to ask if Skittle and Pinch could stay the night. Captain Spoons told Admiral Bonnet, who was only listening with one ear as she was too worried to listen with two. Being worried is a bit like having a fog in the brain, you can't think about anything else.

It seemed to Admiral Bonnet that the fog was steering the island, and that, she thought, most definitely should not be happening.

'I have been thinking,' said Captain Spoons. 'This is the season of driftsea and as we know, it brings strange and wonderful things. But surely it can't have brought the moon, that seems most unlikely. I mean, we would have heard a splash and a rumble. Rubbish Island would have been rocked from side to side. It would have been worse than when Bottle Mountain fell into the sea.'

'I hadn't thought of that,' said Admiral Bonnet. 'Perhaps Ethel B Dina may be wrong about the moon, but right about the Gupper fog.'

It was moontide, which is midnight to the Long Legs and Little Long Legs,

when Spokes and Barnacle Bow left
Ethel's house. Spokes said he would walk
Barnacle Bow home as it was a dark
foggy night, although it didn't take them
long to get lost.

That moontide the fog felt wetter than
it had before.

'If I didn't know better, I would say the
fog is weeping,' said Barnacle Bow.

'Perhaps you are right,' said Spokes.
'Fogs can be discombobulating.'

'You can say that again,' said Barnacle
Bow.

'Discombobulating dampness,' said
Spokes.

'I remember many a jolly rain cloud,' said Barnacle Bow, 'and some rather grumpy sunny days.'

'What about wind?' said Spokes. 'Wind can be bad-tempered and furious as well as gentle as a breeze.'

'Two trees short of a forest, that's how tricky the weather can be,' said Barnacle Bow.

'And we haven't even mentioned rainbows,' said Spokes.

'Upside-down smiles in the sky,' said Barnacle Bow.

That is when they felt a tap on their shoulders.

'Was that you?' asked Barnacle Bow.

'No,' said Spokes. 'Did you tap my shoulder?'

'No, I didn't,' said Barnacle Bow.

They both turned around but could see nothing.

'This fog makes it so hard to see where we are going,' said Spokes, tripping over a stone.

At that moment, the fog cleared, or rather, a path in the fog cleared, so they could see their way to Granny Gull's houseboat.

Both of them hurried as fast as their Tindim legs would take them. Just before they reached the houseboat the fog came back down again.

It sounded as if someone was crying in the fog. Whoever it was sounded sad and wet.

'Hello,' called Spokes. 'Who's there?'

'Me.'

Barnacle Bow held tight to Spokes and Spokes held on even tighter to Barnacle Bow.

'Who is Me?' they both said.

And that is when the sad, wet thing said, 'It's me, the fog, and no one wants me. Not the squid, not the island and not you Tindims. All I want, all I've ever wanted, is a home to cling to.'

Chapter Eight

Where that neeptide
all the news is about
the Gupper fog and
Ethel B Dina goes to
talk to the squid.

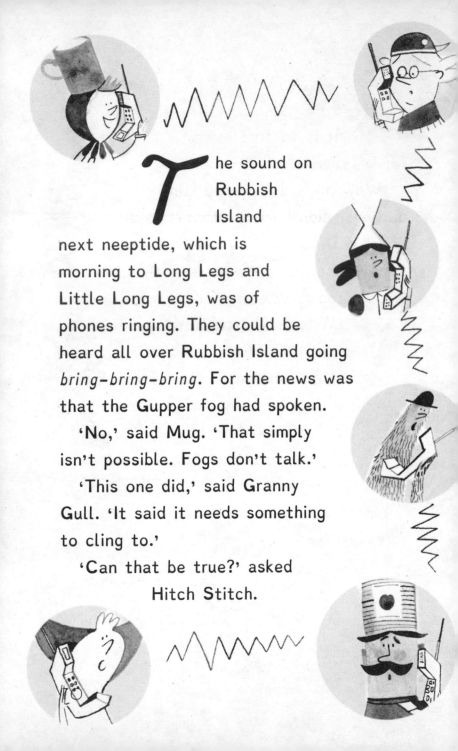

The sound on Rubbish Island next neeptide, which is morning to Long Legs and Little Long Legs, was of phones ringing. They could be heard all over Rubbish Island going *bring-bring-bring*. For the news was that the Gupper fog had spoken.

'No,' said Mug. 'That simply isn't possible. Fogs don't talk.'

'This one did,' said Granny Gull. 'It said it needs something to cling to.'

'Can that be true?' asked Hitch Stitch.

'It is as true as my fur is green,' said Broom.

'Why, my still and sparkling darlings, didn't I know that?' said Ethel B Dina.

'Because, my old lifesaver, the Gupper fog is neither a squid nor a fish,' said Captain Spoons.

'You mean it spoke with real words?' said Brew.

'Will it go away now?' asked Skittle.

'I don't know,' said Admiral Bonnet. 'We can only hope.'

Baby Cup cooed, 'Gup-per, gup-per.'

Ethel decided the best way to get a squid's attention was to sing.

'The squid must know quite a lot about the Gupper fog,' said Ethel. 'It might even know how to make it go away.'

Ethel B Dina put on her red waterproof mac and her brand-new apple green lifesaver ring. She put on her waterproof hat and waterproof boots, all of which had been made out of bits of plastic that had washed up in Turtle Bay.

When she was quite ready she took her handmade waterproof umbrella and opened the front door to find the fog had gone. But where had it gone? She didn't believe it would have just disappeared in the flick of a fish's tail. No, she had a strong feeling it might be hiding somewhere.

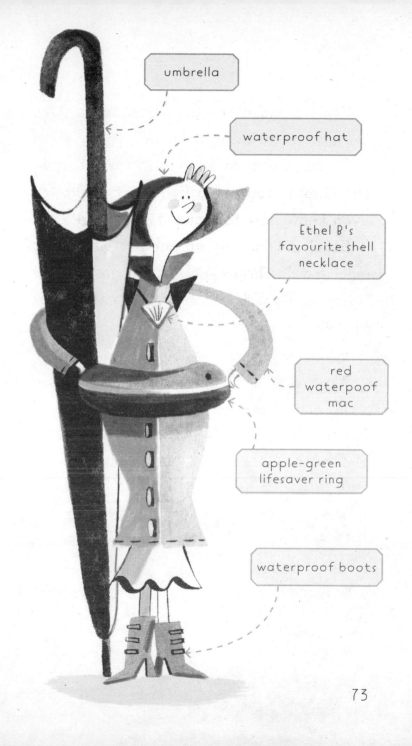

umbrella

waterproof hat

Ethel B's favourite shell necklace

red waterpoof mac

apple-green lifesaver ring

waterproof boots

73

She arrived at the Lake of Still
Waters and was glad not to see the fog
anywhere. 'Good riddance to bad fog,'
she said out loud. Then she put up her
umbrella, took a deep breath and started
to sing. She stopped when she saw
Skittle, Pinch and Brew running towards
her with a hop, a skip and a jump.

'The fog has gone away, now is the day
for play,' said Pinch.

'Yes,' said Ethel. 'Let's hope so.'

It was lovely to see the island once
again. Even Bottle Hill had a rosy glow.

'Now,' said Skittle, 'things can get back to how they were.'

'That's just the ticket,' said Brew. 'We can play in the treehouse again.'

Ethel B Dina got ready to sing.

Skittle said, 'I don't want to pop your bubble of happy thoughts, but do you see what I see in the corner of the lake?'

'Oh, it's the Gupper fog,' said Brew.
'What is it doing there?'

'A good question,' said Ethel. 'Is it
trying to catch the squid?'

Chapter Nine

Where Ethel B Dina
tries to talk to the
luminous squid. And
the Gupper fog is
up to no good.

They watched as the Gupper fog started to tiptoe across the surface of the lake. It made itself into the shape of hundreds of foggy water lilies.

'That is rather magical,' said Brew, holding tight to his wooden spoon.

Wooden spoons are important to Brew. He secretly believes they are magic wands. He doesn't tell many Tindims, only Skittle and Pinch, his best friends, but most of them seem to know. Perhaps they remember Brew's speech at the last Brightsea Festival, where his costume won first prize, and he told everyone his magic wooden spoon had helped.

Ethel B Dina kneeled by the edge of
the lake and started to talk in Squid,
which is a difficult language, with lots of
squiggle sounds and lots of toots.

'Ah,' said Ethel. 'The fog is trying to
trick the squid out of the water and carry
one or other of them away.'

'Why?' asked Skittle.

'I don't know,' said Ethel.

The minute she stood up the Gupper
fog stopped making water lilies. Instead it
spread out and sat on top of the water,
in a rather grumpy sort of way.

Ethel said, 'Never mind. We will have to think of something else.' They were about to leave when a fish poked its head above the surface and spoke to her.

Ethel listened carefully. Now and then saying, 'Yes, I see, of course,' and, 'No, I wouldn't either,' and, 'I was worried about that as well.'

'What is it saying?' asked Skittle.

Ethel B Dina looked vague and said, 'A few years ago, a Gupper fog came to Rubbish Island, bringing with it a squid which it left in the Lake of Still Waters. Now this Gupper fog has also brought a squid to the lake, only this time, the fog isn't leaving. Both squids refuse to come to the surface as they say they are happy down there together. They worry the fog will wrap itself around one or other of them and pull them out of the water and then disappear over the horizon. Both squids agree that would be very sad indeed as they've fallen in love and don't want to be parted.'

'Oh, scrunch me a teabag,' said Brew. 'All that lovey stuff sounds yucky.'

'I am glad I am not a squid or a Gupper fog,' said Skittle.

Ethel B Dina said, 'Our number one thing to do is to protect the squids. Second, we need to send the fog away, and third, and perhaps most important of all, we need to rescue the moon.'

'And *that's a fact actually,*' said Pinch.

Chapter Ten

Where Barnacle Bow goes and asks very nicely if the Gupper fog would please go away. And he and Spokes build a submarine.

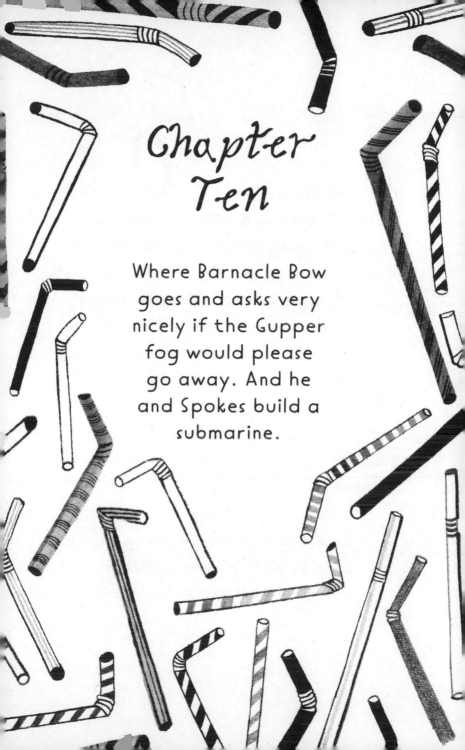

Once
Ethel
B Dina
was back home she phoned
everyone to tell them what
had happened. She said she
thought the best thing would be
for Spokes or Barnacle Bow to try
speaking once again to the Gupper fog
and tell it, in a determined voice, it
had to go.

It was no good. Next day the fog
was as thick as ever it had been, and it
refused to talk to anyone.

Barnacle Bow did his best to explain
that the squids were happy in the
Lake of Still Waters and that
neither wanted to leave.

So, really there was no
need for the Gupper fog to
be on Rubbish Island. Perhaps
it could go home.

The Gupper fog said not a
word, though Barnacle Bow
thought he heard
a moan.

No one was quite sure if it had anything to do with what Barnacle Bow had said to the fog, but perhaps it did. On Winkleday the fog was thicker than ever. So thick you couldn't see your hand in front of your face. Which meant there was no point going outside.

Ethel spent her time at the underwater viewing platform. From there she could see half of the floating moon. More and more luminous fish began to swim from the depths of the sea, attracted by its glowing light.

'This most definitely should not be happening,' said Ethel B Dina to Hitch Stitch on the phone.

There was no getting away from it, something had to be done, and quickly. Every ebbtide Ethel B Dina took a lantern and walked up to Bottle Hill. From there she tried to see the night sky but all she could see was fog.

One thing Ethel knew was that nothing could be right with the world if the moon wasn't king of the night sky.

Brew wondered if the fog might be sulking.

Baby Cup had quite a lot to say on the matter, but no one understood what it was.

A week passed, a rather long and dull week.

Barnacle Bow and Spokes hardly noticed

because they were hard at work designing a submarine. It had to be strong enough to pull the moon out of the sea, that was the tricky part.

The body of the submarine had been made out of the barrel they had found washed up. The plastic dome was attached to the top of the vessel, which meant anyone steering could see where they were going. The rudder they'd found was tied to a wheel so they could drive the submarine.

Barnacle Bow had had a good old rummage in the pile of useful rubbish.

He had been through the 'Useful Rubbish', the 'Nearly Useful Rubbish' and moved onto the 'Might Be Useful Rubbish'.

He had come away with a wheelbarrow full of bits and bobs, wires and knobs and three pram wheels. These, Spokes fitted to the bottom of the submarine so that it would be easy to move around when on dry land.

There were three bicycle lights at the front, which Barnacle Bow thought would help

them see
underwater. And, of
course, he had also fitted a phone
onboard. The whole thing was powered
by a rubber band of double, double
strength and painted with pink and
white stripes.

When Captain Spoons saw it, he
said, 'Trumpets and tin hats. How
are you going to pull the moon out
of the sea with that? I mean,
it has no grabbing claw. In
short, I am not sure it will
work.'

Chapter Eleven

Where Spokes shows
off the main feature
of his submarine and
Broom helps launch it
into the waves.

S pokes had been waiting for this moment to show off the best feature of his design, an easy can't-go-wrong way to get the moon back. At the front of the submarine was a sliding door. If he pushed the yellow button on the control panel, nets (which Hitch Stitch had made) would shoot out and wrap themselves around the floating moon. These would be strong enough to pull it back to Rubbish Island.

'A most impressive invention, but has anyone tried actually sitting inside it?' asked Admiral Bonnet. 'I don't want to dampen your tea towel, but will you fit into such a small space?'

Barnacle Bow and Spokes looked at one another. 'Oh no,' they said together. They had been so busy making the submarine work they hadn't thought of that.

'It's because of all the buttons, knobs and nets,' said Spokes.

Brew went to have a look. 'I could fit inside,' he said. 'And so could Pinch. And,' he added, 'I also happen to be good with switches and buttons as well as wooden spoons.'

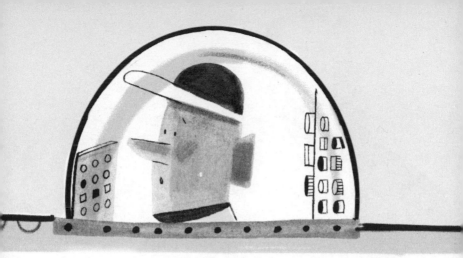

'No, no,' said Admiral Bonnet.

'No,' said Spokes. 'I made this craft with Barnacle Bow and I must be the one to take her out.'

Barnacle Bow opened the small door on the side of the submarine and Spokes squeezed in.

'It's all right,' he said once inside.

Barnacle Bow wasn't so sure.

Spokes said there was nothing to worry about and they wheeled the submarine down to the water.

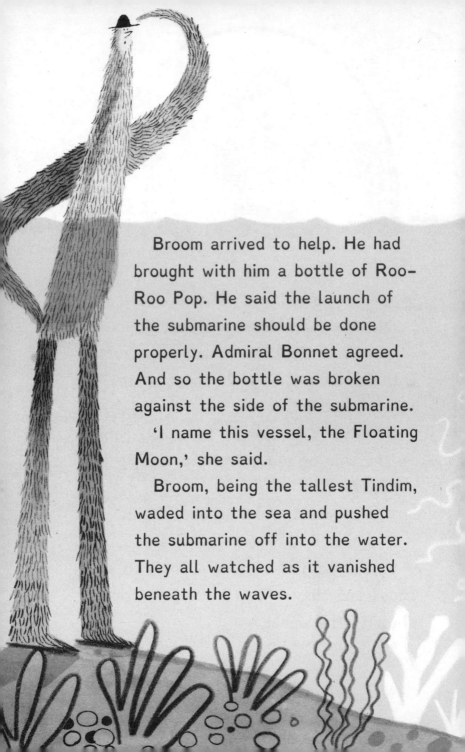

Broom arrived to help. He had brought with him a bottle of Roo-Roo Pop. He said the launch of the submarine should be done properly. Admiral Bonnet agreed. And so the bottle was broken against the side of the submarine.

'I name this vessel, the Floating Moon,' she said.

Broom, being the tallest Tindim, waded into the sea and pushed the submarine off into the water. They all watched as it vanished beneath the waves.

'Oh, blasted nautical maps,' said Admiral Bonnet. 'We forgot a poem. We always have a poem to launch a vessel.'

The Tindims are very fond of poems and songs.

Barnacle Bow said, 'I don't have one.'

'But I do,' said Ethel B Dina. And she began to sing,

'Oh, moon of Tindims' hopes and dreams. We are rescuing you with our submarine.'

Chapter Twelve

Where Spokes finds himself in a bit of a pickle among all the deep-sea fish.

U nder the sea, even with the
lights on, it was hard to see
which way to go. Spokes looked
out of the plastic dome and he could see
all sorts of fish he had never seen before.
The further down he went, the more the
fish seemed to light up, and the bigger
and the stranger they became.

This was a bit of a problem. Spokes
had thought he would only need to
follow the light of the moon, but now the
light from these odd, luminous fish was
confusing him.

When at last he saw the moon, Spokes
realised that the submarine's rubber band
engine seemed to be running out of power.

'There is only one thing to do,' said
Spokes firmly.

With the last burst of energy left
in the engine, he brought the vessel
as close to the moon as possible. Then
he pressed the big yellow button. Just
as Spokes had planned, the nets shot
out and wrapped themselves around
the moon. Except now, he had no power
left to get back to shore. He phoned
Barnacle Bow to tell him he was in
a pickle.

That's when things went from worse
to decidedly wrong. The moon, Spokes
and the submarine started to spin around
and around in a whirl of light and the
whole caboodle began to sink further
into the sea.

There was nothing Spokes could do.
The phone line went dead. He said to
himself, 'Where there is a Tindim, there is
always a way out of any problem.'

He thought of Brew with his wooden
spoons, if there was magic in them, now
would be a good time to use it. Down and
down he went to where the fishes became
even stranger and brighter.

Chapter Thirteen

Where Granny Gull knows
what to do for the
best and she gives an
invitation for tea.

Back on dry land Barnacle Bow was in a bit of a tizz.

'Have you spoken to Spokes?' asked Granny Gull.

'The phone isn't working,' he said. 'I don't know what to do. Panic, I suppose?'

'Panic never got anyone anywhere,' said Granny Gull.

'Everything all right?' asked Mug.

And to everyone's surprise Baby Cup said, 'No, no, no.' She wriggled free from Mug's arms, crawled over to the sand and started making coo-coo noises at the fog.

Suddenly the fog cleared and gathered itself into the shape of an elephant. It went and sat beside Baby Cup.

'I think,' said Granny Gull, 'one of the reasons the fog is being so difficult is that we are not very nice to it. We are always asking it to go away, instead of asking what we can do to help.'

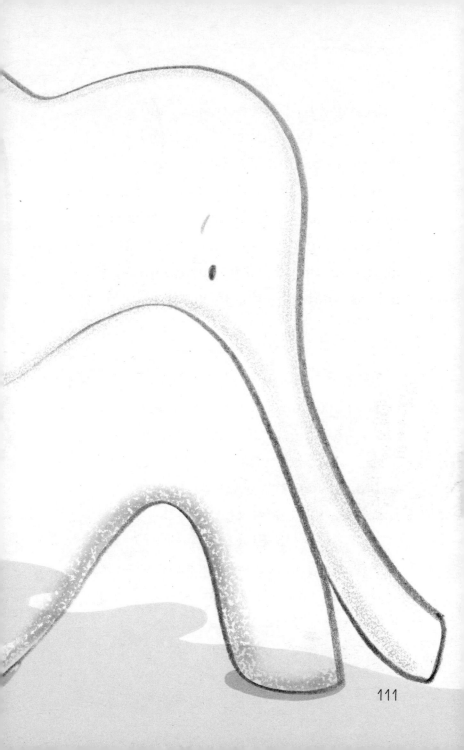

111

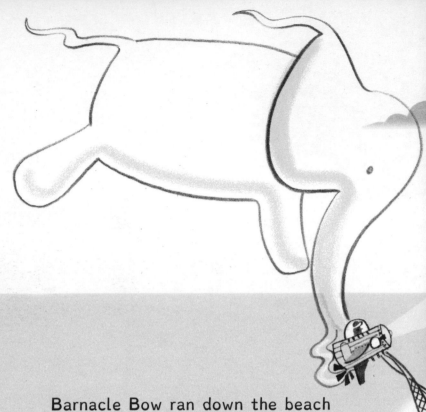

Barnacle Bow ran down the beach
to where the foggy elephant and
Baby Cup were sitting. By now they
could all see the light of the moon
disappearing under the waves.

'Oh no,' said Skittle.

All the Tindims stood on the shore
watching, knowing there was nothing they
could do to help Spokes.

The Gupper fog, without being
told, knew what had happened and
knew what to do. In the shape of an
elephant, it spread out over the sea.
As it went, it grew in size until it was
ginormous. First it raised its trunk high
into the air and then plunged it down,
deep under the foaming water.

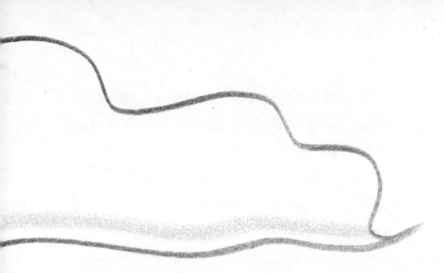

From the beach, the Tindims watched
in amazement as the elephant's tummy
grew bigger and bigger until it was all
lil up and glittering. It brought its trunk
out of the water and began gliding back
to shore.

The Tindims held their breath.

The foggy elephant began to change
again. Now in the shape of a cloud it
lifted into the sky, and there, lying
safely on the beach, was the submarine
and a huge glitter ball. Which, on closer
inspection, looked nothing like the moon.

Barnacle Bow quickly opened the
submarine's door and pulled out a very
shaken Spokes.

'You did it. You are back,' said
Barnacle Bow, hugging his dear friend.

The Tindims danced for
joy until Granny Gull said,
'Wait, look.'

The Gupper fog was moving
slowly away.

'Mr Gupper Fog,' said Granny
Gull, 'where are you going?'

'Nowhere,' said the Gupper fog.
'I have no home. I just live on
top of the sea, hoping a luminous
squid might need me.'

'That rhymes,' said Pinch.

'Mr Gupper Fog,' said Granny Gull, 'we want to thank you.' She looked at the huge glitter ball lying on the beach. 'I am sure it's hollow. While it may not be the moon perhaps it could be a home for you to cling to.'

'For me?' asked the Gupper fog. 'You mean I could live in it and you wouldn't mind?'

'No, of course not,' said the Tindims.

It was agreed by each and every Tindim. It was a perfect idea.

'And would you like to have tea with us?' asked Granny Gull.

'Oh, thank you,' said the Gupper fog. 'I thought you would never ask. I could put on a show for you tomorrow night. I am sure the squids will help me once they know I am not going to carry one of them away.'

'Tomorrow it is,' said Granny Gull. 'But now it's time for tea.'

They set off for home, Barnacle Bow
and Spokes trying to wheel the submarine
up the beach.

'Let me help,' said the Gupper fog and
it picked up the glitter ball in one foggy
arm and the submarine in the other.

'Look,' said Pinch and he pointed to
the sky.

It was the first time in ages that they had been able to see the sky. They looked up and there it was.

'Oh,' said Ethel. 'The moon is back with the stars.'

The Gupper fog began to sing in a lovely deep voice.

'Shine on, shine on, oh, moon of light.
Safe in your star cloth of the night.
There you are above the world so high.
The largest glitter ball in the sky.'

Chapter Fourteen

Where Ethel B Dina, the
Gupper fog and the
squids put on a show,
and what a show it is.

The sun shone brightly and the Tindims were once more at Turtle Bay to see what the driftsea had brought them.

'It's a feast of surprises,' said Hitch Stitch.

They went to work doing what Tindims do best, turning rubbish into treasure. Soon Turtle Bay was as clean as a whistle.

'Where are Spokes
and Barnacle Bow?'
asked Skittle.

'They are on
Bottle Hill.'

'Why?' asked
Pinch.

'Because,' said
Granny Gull,
'they are making
the Gupper fog a
home.'

Skittle, Pinch
and Brew went off
to find them.

Barnacle Bow and
Spokes were at
the top of Bottle
Hill, where the
huge glitter ball
now sat like a
beacon of light.
'What do
you think?' said
Spokes when he
saw them.
Spokes had
made a doorway in
the glitter ball.

Brew knocked and the
Gupper fog asked them all in.

'Look,' said the Gupper
fog. 'I have a home,
finally a place where I
am wanted. Oh, what
a magical day. Now
if you'll excuse me I
have rehearsal with
the squids and Ethel
B Dina.'

The Gupper
fog waved a
happy goodbye
and wafted away.

That ebbtide, the Tindims of Rubbish
Island were all to be found seated on
chairs by the edge of the Lake of Still
Waters. Up on the hill the glitter ball
shone down on them. Each Tindim held a

lantern and they watched, amazed, as the
Gupper fog wrapped itself around Ethel
B Dina and floated to the middle of the
lake, which was lit by the squids.

Ethel began to sing:

'I see the moon and the moon sees me,
Down through the leaves of the Roo-Roo tree.

Floating moon, shine over the sea.
By the light of the moon, I will dance with thee.'

The Gupper fog turned itself into a
bird and then into a dragon that roared.

130

Finally, the fog made itself into the shape of a heart and sang the last verse in its beautiful, deep voice:

'To Rubbish Island over the sea,
Back to the lake, where I long to be,
In my glitter ball, on the hill above,
Singing the Gupper's song of love.'

Chapter Fifteen

Where everything is just as it should be with the Tindims and Rubbish Island.

I am now taking a well earned rest. See you all next driftsea!

The Gupper fog loved its new home. Rubbish Island felt proud it had chosen to stay and by the time driftsea had passed the Gupper fog yawned and went off to bed.

It hung a notice on the glitter ball which read, 'I am now taking a well-earned rest. See you all next driftsea.'

Occasionally they could see the
fog's dreams as it slept in its glitter
ball. It would build castles in the sky
and sometimes they could see it
counting sheep.

Soon no one could remember a time
when they didn't have the Gupper fog
living on the island. Some nights when the
sky was bright, and the stars shone down,
they could hear it singing.

On those nights the Tindims slept and snored well.

Pinch would like to add a word by saying, 'Remember, rubbish today is treasure tomorrow.' And Skittle wants to say that they are all very pleased the Gupper fog found a home.

'That's what everyone needs,' said Brew. 'As well as a wooden spoon.'

'And *that's a fact actually*,' said Pinch.

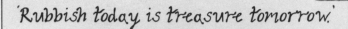

'Rubbish today is treasure tomorrow.'

PLASTIC BOTTLE MARACAS

* Fill a plastic bottle with anything that will make a sound when shaken — maybe dried peas or beans.

* Take a toilet roll tube and cut halfway up one side.

* Fit toilet roll snugly over top of bottle and use sticky tape to attach it.

* You can then paint or decorate your maracas.

Make a pair of maracas and join in with the Tindims!

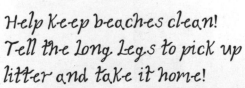

Help keep beaches clean!
Tell the long Legs to pick up
litter and take it home!